the story behind a favorite christmas song

the 12 DAYS of CHRISTMAS

Written by Helen Haidle
Illustrated by Laura Knorr

ZONDERVAN.com/
AUTHORTRACKER
follow your favorite authors

ZONDERKIDZ

The 12 Days of Christmas

Requests for information should be addressed to:

Zonderkidz, *Grand Rapids, Michigan 49530*

ISBN 978-0-310-72283-0

Printed in China

18 19 20 21 22 /DSC/ 23 22 21 20 19 18 17 16 15 14 13 12 11 10 9 8 7 6 5

With love and much appreciation to my friend,
Toni Von Hollen, creative storyteller extraordinaire.
Thanks for your encouragement to find out the history
behind this song and write a book about it.
May the Lord richly bless you
and your husband, Richard, and daughter, Marissa.
—H.H.

To my husband, Mark, my true love.
—L.K.

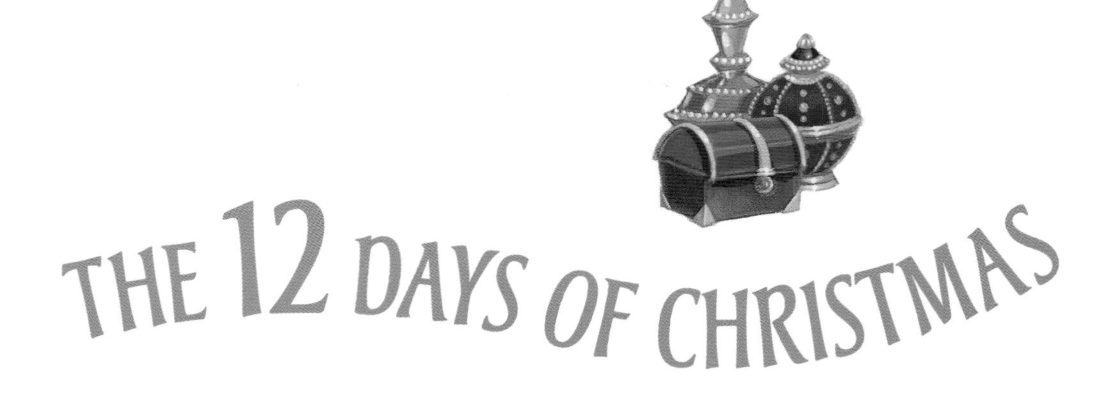

THE 12 DAYS OF CHRISTMAS

Many years ago, people wanted a day on which to celebrate Jesus' birthday. Finally, three hundred and fifty years after Jesus was born, December 25 was selected as "Christ-mass," the day for his birthday party.

The twelfth day after Christmas, January 6, was selected as the day to honor the visit of the wise men to Jesus. This day was called Epiphany (e-piff-an-ee). In 567 A.D., the twelve days between Christmas and Epiphany were filled with festivals, ending with a party on the Twelfth Night.

Let's take a look at a song about twelve gifts given on each of those twelve days of Christmas.

MY TRUE LOVE

No one really knows when or why the song "The Twelve Days of Christmas" was written. The legend is that during the sixteenth century, the officials of the Church of England forbade all other religious teaching about Christ except theirs. So for the next two hundred years, parents who refused to join this church used the song to teach their children in secret.

Let's discover the twelve Christian meanings hidden in the gifts of this song. But first of all, let's find out who gives the gifts. The song calls this giver "My True Love." Who could that person be? Who loves you and gives you many things each day?

Well, the only one who does all that is God!

Every good and perfect gift
is from above.
James 1:17

A PARTRIDGE IN A PEAR TREE

On the first day of Christmas, my True Love gave to me
a partridge in a pear tree.

What is the first (and best) gift in this song?

Do you know what a partridge is? It is a small bird that looks like a little brown chicken. This brave bird is willing to give its life to defend its babies from harm.

Who does the partridge remind you of? Think of the one person who willingly gave his life for you. Jesus! And remember what a cross was made from—a tree.

So let the partridge in a pear tree remind you of Jesus, the best Christmas gift of all, who died for us on the cross.

For God so loved the world that he gave his one and only Son,
that whoever believes in him shall not perish but have eternal life.

John 3:16

TWO TURTLEDOVES

On the second day of Christmas, my True Love gave to me two turtledoves.

Turtledoves (also called doves) are known as gentle birds of peace. Long ago people gave doves to God as a gift of love. Jewish fathers and mothers gave two doves to God when they brought a newborn baby to the temple in Jerusalem.

Guess what Mary and Joseph gave to God when they took Jesus to the temple when he was a baby? Yes, two turtledoves.

So let the gift of two turtledoves remind you of the two doves given to God when baby Jesus was first brought to the temple.

Joseph and Mary took him to Jerusalem to present him to the Lord . . . and to offer him a sacrifice . . ."a pair of doves . . ."

Luke 2:22, 24

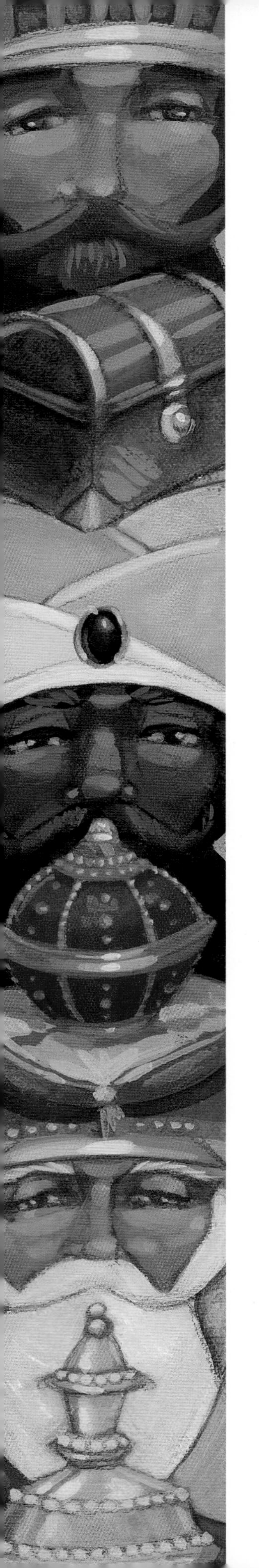

3

THREE FRENCH HENS

On the third day of Christmas, my True Love gave to me three French hens.

Long ago French hens cost a lot more than ordinary chickens. Only wealthy people could buy them.

What could three expensive birds remind you of? Can you think of a Bible story about three important gifts meant for a king? Remember what gifts were given to baby Jesus? The wise men gave him three expensive gifts—gold, incense, and myrrh.

Gold is the most valuable gift of all. Incense comes from tree bark and is burned during times of prayer. Myrrh is a thick reddish gum used as a perfume.

So let the three French hens remind you of three costly gifts given to Jesus by the wise men.

When they saw the star, they were overjoyed. On coming to the house, they saw the child with his mother Mary, and they bowed down and worshiped him. Then they opened their treasures and presented him with gifts of gold, frankincense and myrrh.

Matthew 2:10-11

Trois
Poules
Françaises

FOUR CALLING BIRDS

On the fourth day of Christmas, my True Love gave to me four calling birds.

God created all kinds of birds, each with a special song. Have you heard sparrows chirp or pigeons coo? Have you heard blackbirds shout, "Caw, caw, caw"?

Have you heard of four men named Matthew, Mark, Luke, and John who wrote about Jesus? Each of them had their own story to tell. They were like calling birds because the books they wrote called people to believe in Jesus.

So let the four calling birds remind you of Matthew, Mark, Luke, and John and the four special books they wrote.

But these are written that you may
believe that Jesus is the Messiah, the Son of God.

John 20:31

5

FIVE GOLDEN RINGS

On the fifth day of Christmas, my True Love gave to me five golden rings.

Gold rings are some of the most treasured of all gifts. Do you know someone who wears a gold ring?

Jewish people consider the first five books of the Old Testament—the Torah or the Law (God's directions)—to be five great treasures worth more than gold. Can you name these five books? They tell many stories of God, Adam, Eve, Noah, Joseph, and Moses.

So let the five golden rings remind you of five valuable books of the Bible: Genesis, Exodus, Leviticus, Numbers, and Deuteronomy.

The decrees of the LORD are firm, and all of them are righteous.
They are more precious than gold, than much pure gold.

Psalm 19:9-10

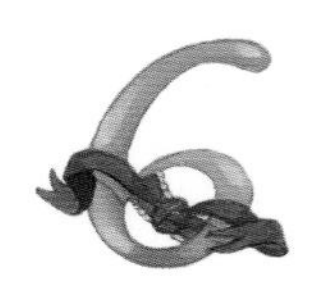

SIX GEESE A-LAYING

On the sixth day of Christmas, my True Love gave to me six geese a-laying.

Do you know what people in China used to hand out when a new baby was born? They gave an egg to each of their friends! Why do you think they gave an egg? Remember what is inside of each egg: a new life—a baby chick.

Where does the Bible tell about six days of new life? The first two chapters of the book of Genesis tell how God made plants, birds, fish, animals, a man, and a woman.

So let the six geese laying eggs remind you of the new life God made in the first six days of creation.

God saw all that he had made,
and it was very good . . . the sixth day.

Genesis 1:31

SEVEN SWANS A-SWIMMING

On the seventh day of Christmas, my True Love gave to me seven swans a-swimming.

Have you ever seen a new baby swan? When it first hatches, the swan is black. It looks like an ugly duckling. As it grows and changes, it becomes more beautiful. Its neck stretches out, and its feathers turn snowy white.

How do you grow as God's child? The Holy Spirit changes you on the inside—in your heart and in your mind. The Holy Spirit gives seven special gifts to God's children. These gifts help us to grow and serve others.

So let seven swimming swans remind you of the seven gifts of the Holy Spirit.

We have different gifts, according to the grace given to each of us. If your gift is prophesying, then prophesy in accordance with your faith; if it is serving, then serve; if it is teaching, then teach; if it is to encourage, then give encouragement; if it is giving, then give generously; if it is to lead, do it diligently; if it is to show mercy, do it cheerfully.

Romans 12:6-8

EIGHT MAIDS A-MILKING

On the eighth day of Christmas, my True Love gave to me eight maids a-milking.

What food do all babies need in order to grow? Milk helps your bones grow strong and healthy like God wants you to be.

Do you know how reading God's Word in the Bible is like drinking milk? God's Word helps you grow in your heart and mind and spirit. Jesus taught his followers eight special sayings called the Beatitudes to help them grow strong in their faith.

So let eight maids a-milking remind you of the eight Beatitudes.

"Blessed are the poor in spirit, for theirs is the kingdom of heaven.
Blessed are those who mourn, for they will be comforted.
Blessed are the meek, for they will inherit the earth.
Blessed are those who hunger and thirst for righteousness, for they will be filled.
Blessed are the merciful, for they will be shown mercy.
Blessed are the pure in heart, for they will see God.
Blessed are the peacemakers, for they will be called children of God.
Blessed are those who are persecuted because of righteousness, for theirs is the kingdom of heaven."

Matthew 5:3-10

NINE LADIES DANCING

On the ninth day of Christmas, my True Love gave to me nine ladies dancing.

Are you a happy person? Do you ever dance when you feel joyful? Do you know people who need more joy in their lives, or more love or peace or patience? How does a person get all these things?

God's Holy Spirit is our helper. He makes love, joy, peace, patience, kindness, goodness, faithfulness, gentleness, and self-control grow inside of us. Those are good reasons to dance for joy!

So let nine ladies dancing remind you of the nine qualities that God's Holy Spirit produces in your life.

But the fruit of the Spirit is love, joy, peace, forbearance, kindness, goodness, faithfulness, gentleness and self-control.

Galatians 5:22-23

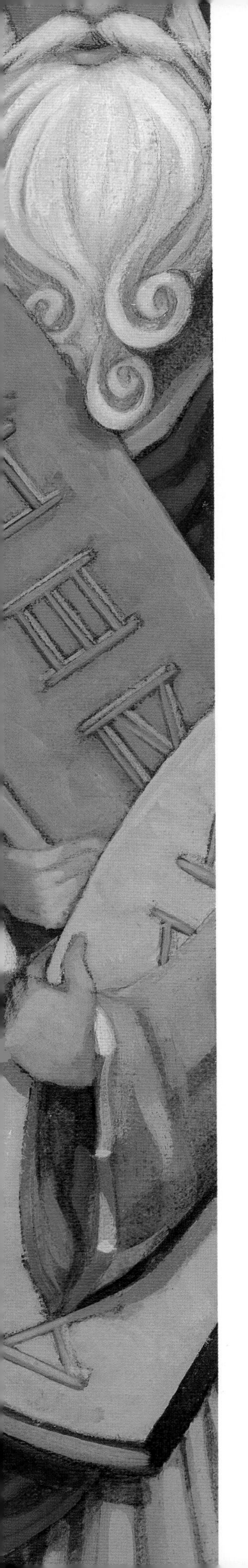

10

TEN LORDS A-LEAPING

On the tenth day of Christmas, my True Love gave to me ten lords a-leaping.

Long ago lords were important men whose commands had to be obeyed. People honored lords and obeyed their rules.

Whose rules do you obey? Do you know the ten important rules God asks us to follow? The Ten Commandments tell us what to do and what not to do. They show us how to love God and other people.

So let the ten leaping lords remind you of the Ten Commandments, which we are to obey.

"I am the LORD your God...
You shall have no other gods before me.
You shall not make for yourself an image in the form of anything...
You shall not bow down to them or worship them.
You shall not misuse the name of the LORD your God...
Remember the Sabbath day by keeping it holy...
Honor your father and your mother...
You shall not murder. You shall not commit adultery. You shall not steal.
You shall not give false testimony against your neighbor.
You shall not covet... anything that belongs to your neighbor."

Exodus 20:2-17

ELEVEN PIPERS PIPING

On the eleventh day of Christmas, my True Love gave to me eleven pipers piping.

Years ago a piper was a man who traveled through villages playing happy tunes on his flute-pipe. What do you think happened when children heard his music? They followed him all over town!

Twelve disciples followed Jesus everywhere he went, but only eleven faithfully stayed with him. Judas double-crossed Jesus. Like pipers, the eleven disciples piped the song of God's love everywhere they went. Many people listened to their message and followed Jesus too.

So let eleven pipers piping help you remember to follow Jesus.

These are the twelve he appointed: Peter... James...
and his brother John, Andrew, Philip, Bartholomew, Matthew,
Thomas, James son of Alphaeus, Thaddaeus, Simon the Zealot
and Judas Iscariot, who betrayed him.

Mark 3:16-19

12

TWELVE DRUMMERS DRUMMING

On the twelvth day of Christmas, my True Love gave to me twelve drummers drumming.

What is a drummer's special job? A drummer must beat out a steady rhythm so everyone can march or play music together in unity. What would happen if drummers stopped drumming?

Christians belong to many different churches, but one thing gives them unity—their common beliefs. The Apostles' Creed lists twelve things Christians believe about God. This brings oneness and unity, like a band marching to the drummers' beat.

So let twelve drummers drumming remind you of The Apostles' Creed—twelve important beliefs of Christians.

The Apostles' Creed

I believe in God the Father Almighty, maker of heaven and earth.
I believe in Jesus Christ, his only Son, our Lord,
who was conceived by the Holy Spirit and born of the Virgin Mary.
He suffered under Pontius Pilate, was crucified, died, and was buried.
He descended into hell; the third day he rose from the dead.
He ascended into heaven and sits at the right hand of God the Father.
He shall return to judge both the living and the dead.
I believe in the Holy Spirit, the holy Christian Church, the communion of saints,
the forgiveness of sins, the resurrection of the body, and the life everlasting.